Richard Scarry's

Things to Love

A GOLDEN BOOK • NEW YORK

Western Publishing Company, Inc., Racine, Wisconsin 53404

ISBN: 0-307-11818-5/ISBN: 0-307-61818-8 (lib. bdg.)   ABCDEFGHIJ

Maud loves Brambles.

Mother loves Babykins.

Fingers loves Ozzie.

Kitty loves Pickles.

Mose loves to wear hats.
When he takes them off, Babykins
has fun building a tall tower.

Fingers loves to be
photographed. Just look
at that big smile.

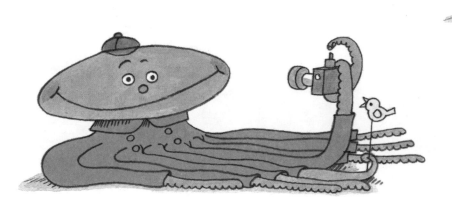

Brambles is such a handsome
fellow. He loves to look at
himself in the mirror.

Whoopee! Here comes the cake.
Come down from there, Squeaky. We know
how you love cake.

The children love to eat
foods like ice cream...

cheese...

carrot...

and watermelon.

Do you have a favorite
food you love to eat?

Tom and his friends love to make music.

The chicks love to sing
along with the music.

Big Hilda and her friends
love to dance to the music.
Don't you love to sing
and dance, too?

The children love to play
games like jacks...

marbles...

throwing bean bags...

hopscotch...

tag...

croquet...

and checkers.

What games do you love?

Babykins loves to be naughty.
He loves to pour his cereal
over his head…

throw his toys
out of his playpen…

run away from
Mother at bathtime…

tease Daddy...

and make loud music.
What a naughty baby. Oh, well. Babies are like that.

Babykins loves to see the children in their costumes at Halloween. He wishes he were big enough to go with them. Soon he will be.

The children love to go shopping with their mothers.

Then the piglets have lots
of fun helping Mother Pig
cook the food that she bought
at the market.

It's so exciting to go to the circus!
The children shout and clap with delight.
The band is playing, and the acrobats
and animals are doing their acts.

Look at everyone happily working in the garden.
They love to dig, plant, and weed.

Mother enjoys picking
the pretty flowers
growing there.

It's a beautiful day, and Mother Pig is taking the Pig family for a drive in the country.

Whoopee! Fresh corn for sale. How the Pigs love fresh corn.

FRESH CORN

It's delightful to have a picnic in the country, with lots of buttery
fresh corn to eat. How delicious!

Look! Do you see who have invited themselves to the Pig family picnic?

Squiggles and Flossie love to go to the library. Surprise! Squiggles has found a book about himself. A librarian is helping Flossie find a book she can take home to read.

What a wonderful way
to end a very nice day.
Mother is reading Hannibal
his favorite bedtime story.
Good night, Hannibal.
Good night, Squeaky.
We love you.